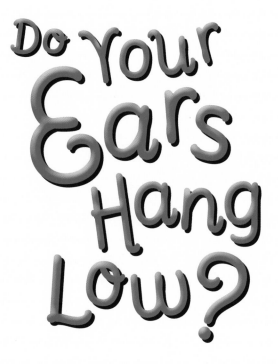

This book belongs to:

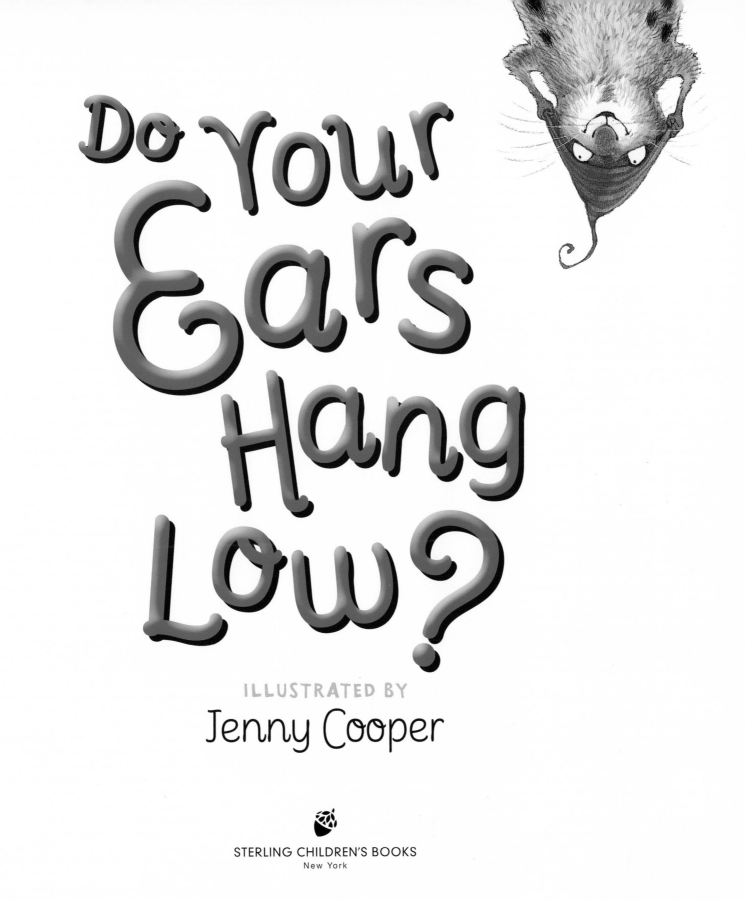

Do Your Ears Hang Low?

ILLUSTRATED BY

Jenny Cooper

STERLING CHILDREN'S BOOKS
New York

Do your ears hang low?
Do they wobble to and fro?

Can you tie them in a knot?

Can you tie them in a bow?

Can you throw them o'er your shoulder like a continental soldier?

Do your ears hang low?

Do your ears
stand high?

Do they reach up to the sky?

Do they droop when they are wet?

Do they stiffen
when they're dry?

Can you wave them at
your neighbor

with a minimum
of labor?

Do your ears
stand high?

Do your ears flip-flop?
Can you use them as a mop?

Are they stringy at the bottom?

Are they curly at the top?

Can you use them for a swatter?

Can you use them for a blotter?

Do your ears flip-flop?

Do your ears stick out?
Can you waggle them about?

blaaaa
blaa
blaaaaaa
blaaaa
blaaaaaa
blaaaaaaa
blaaaaaa
blaaaaaa
blaaaaaa
blaaaaaa
blaaaaaa

Can you shut them up for sure when you hear an awful bore?

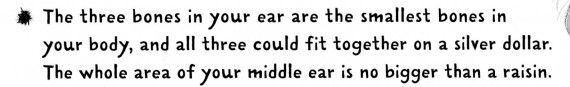

* The three bones in your ear are the smallest bones in your body, and all three could fit together on a silver dollar. The whole area of your middle ear is no bigger than a raisin.

* Cobras in snake-charming acts are responding to the sight of the flute, not its sound.

* A cat has 32 muscles in each ear, and each ear can turn independently.

* Cicadas have their "ears" in their abdomen, and grasshoppers and crickets have them in their knees!

STERLING CHILDREN'S BOOKS
New York

An Imprint of Sterling Publishing Co., Inc.
1166 Avenue of the Americas
New York, NY 10036

This Sterling edition published in 2017 under license from Scholastic Australia Pty Limited
on behalf of Scholastic New Zealand Limited
First published in 2012 by Scholastic New Zealand Limited

ISBN 978-1-4549-1614-7

Distributed in Canada by Sterling Publishing
c/o Canadian Manda Group, 664 Annette Street
Toronto, Ontario, Canada M6S 2C8

For information about custom editions, special sales, and premium and corporate purchases,
please contact Sterling Special Sales at 800-805-5489 or specialsales@sterlingpublishing.com.

Manufactured in China
Lot #:
2 4 6 8 10 9 7 5 3 1
12/16

www.sterlingpublishing.com

Illustrations created in 2B pencil, watercolor paint, some acrylic paint,
and about 10 really, really small paintbrushes!